I0713405

Night Visitors

Lilly Maytree

LIGHTSMITH PUBLISHERS

Thorne Bay, Alaska

LIGHTSMITH PUBLISHERS
P.O. Box 19293
Thorne Bay, AK 99919
www.LightsmithPublishers.com

Quantity sales ordering information:

Special discounts are available on quantity purchases by corporations, associations, and others. For details, contact the "Special Sales Department" at the address above.

Night Visitors/ Lilly Maytree.

1st Edition ISBN-13: 978-1-944798-10-9

Published in the United States of America

*"I do not at all understand the mystery of grace—
only that it meets us where we are but does not
leave us where it found us."*

~Anne Lamott

1

Marion Bates had no idea they were coming. During a time in her life when things were better than ever, such an intrusion was absolutely the last thing on her mind. At that particular moment, it seemed she was in her prime, and all her dreams were coming true. Everything had happened so fast...like the flip of a coin.

First, (and in the nick of time) her husband, Bill, received a promotion. Nobody deserved it more after the nineteen years he had given to *Crossgrove Heating and Air*. He had been their top field technician for years. So, when the senior Harry Crossgrove retired, Harry Junior took over and appointed her own wonderful husband as the new vice-president. Of course, the hours were longer but the new pay-scale was fabulous.

They were able to send Sarah to nursing school and sail through William's last two high school football seasons without having to see only the home games. At least, Marion saw them all. Bill had more responsibilities at the company and often had to work late. Something he didn't mind, because it meant the house would be paid off in a little less than ten years, which would open the door for a more comfortable retirement. Instead of the "barely get by" kind.

Yes, things had definitely been looking up, back then.

There was a bump in the road when Sarah married a medical student who later took an internship back east (the opposite side of the country!) and Marion felt like she would probably never see them again. Not living in Portland, Oregon, she wouldn't. But she still had William, who was working toward a scholarship at the local university and might even be talked into living at home for a while to save on expenses. Instead, he joined the military right after graduation and was immediately stationed in Germany.

His enlistment caused Marion to have to navigate her way over yet another bump and out of a terrible case of "empty nest syndrome." Dear, God... now what was she going to do? But she still had her wonderful hard-working husband and their church family over at Trinity Lutheran. She was secretary of the Ladies' Aid Society there and had taught in the Sunday school for nearly twenty years. Fifth and sixth grade, mostly, which was her absolute favorite age to work with. Almost everything about Marion Bates was absolute.

So, it was with absolute abandon that, after still finding herself melancholy in spite of all these things, she took Bill's suggestion of doing something she had never done before. She decided to pursue a writing career. Something she had often dreamed about but never had time for. She heard it took too much hard work and dedication to really make a go of it. But she certainly had time for it, now.

What a surprise it was when she applied for

a job at the *Columbia Herald* newspaper and actually got one. The door opened so easily things felt almost charmed. Before she knew it, she was writing a weekly cooking column (something she knew almost everything about), interviewing fascinating local cooks, hunting down unusual recipes, and loving every minute of it. She even joined a local writers' club. Which she also loved.

Except for that slightly irritating young woman, Dee Parker, who also worked at the newspaper, and seemed to be forever striking up a conversation when Marion was trying to connect with a more interesting guest speaker. Usually with a cup of coffee or bit of dessert Dee had taken upon herself to bring over, so it was practically impossible to refuse. Dee was always so happy to see her, too, as if they were some kind of best friends.

As if she could be best friends with someone nearly half her age who had never even been married yet, nor understood what it was like to raise a family. Why, they didn't even write about the same things. Although, Marion had to admit Dee Parker was an excellent writer, and had even won the *Columbia Herald* Feature Award two years running. Something that never went to her head, which was a real virtue these days.

Marion had coveted that award from the first moment she heard about it. But how rare would it be for the editors to choose some exquisite recipe for Beef Bourguignon developed by a chef who was three-quarters French, over a high-interest scandal piece that had just made headlines. So, unless she was promoted to real news instead of just a cooking column, that was that. She was more interested in writing books, anyway.

So, she threw herself into the research of plot construction, characterization, and writing craft, in the only way she could. Which was her complete, absolute, hundred percent best of everything she had. She even converted her sewing room into a writing room and stayed up until all hours hammering out stories. She took to drinking copious amounts of green tea to "keep the momentum going." But it wasn't nearly enough.

The writing field was a competitive one and it was harder than she thought to get a handle on it. You had to gather your own readers, and to do that you actually had to be somebody people would sit up and take notice of. Even though she had never been that kind of person in her life, Marion wasn't one to give up easily.

Her efforts led to getting one of those new stylish haircuts (that looked more messed up than combed), changing her basic earth-tone wardrobe to colors that had more flash, and buying a new pair of glasses with the latest style in frames. The only real reaction that came after all that effort was from Bill. He said he liked her better the old way. But there is something to be said about quitting anything too soon, and just as she was contemplating returning to her former dignity, she saw a breakthrough.

Mr. Devlin (one of the senior editors for real news) gave her an assignment for a public opinion article on gun control. A very controversial topic. One that could actually make her a contender for next year's feature award, if she did a good enough job on it. At the very least, it could open the door for more news reporting. Which was why Marion Bates was on top of the world, that day.

For about an hour.

She was still celebrating, sitting at a corner table in a nearby coffee bar, sipping on a java chip frappuccino with whipped cream (her favorite) and jotting down a few notes on how she would structure her news story. The cell phone interrupted just as she began a list of possible "big wigs" she might be able to interview who would add more weight to the piece. Like the Mayor, and the Attorney Gen—

That was as far as she got. Attorney Gen— before she said, "Hello?" Thinking, if it was Bill, she would talk him into going out to dinner over at that little Italian place she liked so much, by way of celebration. Only it wasn't Bill. It was Harry Crossgrove Junior, to inform her that Bill seemed to have had "an episode" and she needed to get down to the hospital as soon as possible.

It was an episode that graduated Bill into a whole new realm altogether, because even though he lingered in a coma for nearly two weeks, it was really over at that particular moment. How ironic that he actually left her on what would have been the first day of the first cruise they ever would have taken together. Something they had saved up for ever since the promotion. Dear, God...she prayed what was she going to do?

Marion had a complete meltdown after he was gone and the funeral was a blur. Her kids came home, of course, but it was all such a shock, and they had to leave before she could recover. The pastor and his wife came to ask if there was anything they could pray with her about. She just wanted to have Bill back, but they didn't mention that. Instead they assured her that she would have peace and comfort in the days ahead.

After that, the night visits began.

2

They started gradually, or she would have fought it with everything she had left in her. But, instead, she was tricked into thinking she was just having some prolonged reaction to losing her husband and things would get better over time. At least, that's what everyone told her. Don't make any sudden changes or big decisions during the first year, they said, or she would regret it later on.

That's how it was, when Marion lost her passion for even getting up in the morning (much less pursuing a writing career). She turned in her resignation down at the *Columbia Herald* and took to living in her pajamas for days on end. Which might have turned into weeks and then months, if that annoying Dee Parker hadn't missed her at the next writers' meeting and come knocking at the door to check up on her. It was the middle of an afternoon and she had brought along a java chip frappuccino with whipped cream.

She didn't mention a thing about the pajamas or the wreck of a house Marion once kept up as beautifully as if it had been on call for occasional layovers for dignitaries. She merely looked straight into Marion's eyes with her own friendly blues (that had the longest lashes Marion had ever seen on a woman) and started right into talking as if they had known each other all their lives.

"I tried calling your cell to remind you about the Russian poet, Mare, but you didn't answer."

"I..." Marion took a sip from the straw trying to hedge for an excuse (oh, how delicious!). "I always heard they had a tendency to be morbid, those Russians."

"He couldn't come. But you'll never guess

who did." She sat down on the nearest chair in the living room and began to rummage through a flower print canvas bag that said *American Originals, Inc.* on it. "Miss Wiggy." At which point she pulled out a book that looked to be covered in green velvet with the silhouette of an old mansion on front.

"That famous children's author?"

"It was a big surprise to everyone, let me tell you. And what a character. Came dressed in a hat and cape—like a British nanny, or something— look, I had her sign a book for you."

"For me?"

"Sure, she wrote your name in it."

Marion set her drink on the lamp table, took the little beauty in her own hands, and hurriedly thumbed to the title page, which read: *"Dearest Marion, here's hoping as you pursue your dreams, you will always remember to throw a lifeline out to the little folk, now and then. Your sister of the pen, Miss Wiggy."* Which caused the first breath of life to flutter—like butterfly wings— from somewhere inside Marion that she didn't even know existed anymore.

It was an emotional moment, that she couldn't even begin to express, beyond whispering, "Dearest Marion" a couple of times, and trying to blink back a rush of sudden unexpected tears. Not to mention, her former annoyance with Dee Parker melted away like whipped cream in coffee, and she suddenly believed her to be one of the most thoughtful people she had ever met.

That fast. Like the flip of a coin.

Something Marion assumed would only be like "ships passing in the night" because—other than the emotion of the moment—what did a young, busy reporter like Dee Parker have in common with a middle-aged widow that could sustain any kind of lasting friendship between them? A lot, obviously, because they became the best of friends from that moment on. In spite of all their differences. It really was the strangest thing.

"Shouldn't you be at work?" Marion asked.

"I am at work." Dee reached back into the flowered bag and took out a small notebook and pen. "I got assigned to cover your cooking column until you come back, and—"

"I'm probably never coming back."

"Whatever. Anyway, I decided you'd be the first person I interviewed. Got a favorite recipe you'd like to share?"

"No, I don't think..." Marion stirred the straw around in her glass and took another sip before suddenly looking up with a mild surprise. "You know, I do, actually. My Boston Brown. It makes a fabulous breakfast bread."

Which was the beginning of their first collaboration, and after that, one thing simply led to another. The fact that they were about as opposite as two people could get didn't seem to matter. Marion was a quiet conservative Lutheran, while Dee was the daughter of some wild-eyed evangelist. Marion had never left Portland, and Dee had been helping out missions in foreign countries ever since she was a teenager. And while Marion wanted to write the "great American novel" and get famous, Dee was perfectly content to write newspaper articles and hope that one day she might have a hand in changing even a few of the injustices in the world.

All of which had no bearing, whatsoever, "when the chips were down." Because Dee Parker had a tendency to show up at the right time and place (it was uncanny how she could even know those things), in the nick of time, over and over again. Some places she took to hauling Marion right along with her, as if she couldn't manage the situation without her. At the very least, it had gotten her out of pajamas and back into the real world again. Not to mention how catching the excitement of such a lifestyle could be.

Yes, things were finally looking up for Marion, again... except for the nights.

3

It began with little rustlings, or seeing shadows out of the corner of her eye. She didn't think much of it at first. Everyone knows houses have their own sounds or tendencies to "settle" with creaks and groans. She just never noticed before. They didn't bother her, really, because they were such small things. She was barely even aware of them most of the time.

Nights were the hardest after Bill was gone.

Marion was always one to stay up late working on any number of projects she happened to be enthused about. At the moment it was writing a children's novel. Something that —for the first time since Bill left—she felt truly comfortable doing. It helped that writing had been his suggestion in the first place, and it made her feel closer to him somehow. Not to mention the encouragement she got from Miss Wiggy (Dearest Marion!).

She couldn't remember exactly when she began sleeping in the guest bedroom, except one day she realized it had been a very long time since she had even opened the door on the other one. Then one night when she was passing by she thought she heard something in there and it gave her a start. Any other time she would have gone right in and settled whatever it was. A breeze coming in through a window she had forgotten to close, maybe.

She would have gone in and figured it out in the morning except that was the day the water heater went out, which necessitated calling a repairman and making a trip to the bank to transfer some money out of savings to cover the expense. Finding out she barely had enough left over to buy groceries after that was a complete shock. Where had it all gone? Between some insurance money and what they had saved up for their vacation, she was sure she could get by for a long time. Why, she was practically destitute!

She should have gone back to work, but she had the nagging sense she wasn't up to it yet. Not when the slightest thing could still send her into an embarrassing crying jag that might last for hours. She had to do something, though. Bothering her kids was out of the question. Young people had a hard enough time making ends meet these days. And it would be a terrible thing to have to admit.

Dear, God... what was she going to do?

How Dee Parker got wind of it, she never knew. It just seemed like she was forever bringing "take out" over from some favorite restaurant when Marion would have opened a can of soup or fixed noodles that day. The truth was, Marion could have probably lived a good six months on just the canned goods she had in her pantry (she was a firm believer in disaster preparedness) but that kind of fare had little appeal on a long-term basis.

Especially without a disaster. Still, the fact that she had allowed herself to get into the situation made her feel a terrible sense of disappointment. Something that dropped her self-image quotient to an all-time low. The last straw came when she realized a great portion of those rustlings and shadows she thought had been the forerunners of losing her mind, were nothing more than an infestation of mice. Which should have given her a great sense of relief, except that she absolutely hated mice.

It was like having someone forever sneaking around, hollering "Boo!" at the most inopportune times. This led to frequent ear-splitting screams that would have concerned the neighbors if they lived any closer or happened to be in their yard at just the right time. She was also letting herself go in such a way that would prove a terrible habit to break later on, if she ever wanted to be normal, again. But at the time, she didn't care.

About anything.

Not even her own house, which was the

absolute last thing she had in the world. At that point she could have sold the thing. Would have jumped at the chance, except the market was down and she would barely make any profit. Especially after paying off the second they had taken out last year to put in a covered patio with a built-in brick barbecue. However, it did lead to the idea to rent out one of her rooms.

To one of the university students, maybe. Except she would have to clean herself up and at least stop screaming at every little thing that bothered her, or they'd think she was deranged. Was she losing her mind? Well, maybe she was. A shock like the loss of a husband had been known to do that to people. Look what it did to Mary Lincoln.

She was wondering how much she could rent a room for—if it would even be worth the bother—when something extremely unusual happened. She typed, "room with a private bath" into a search box of the *Columbia Herald* online classified section without thinking to navigate to ad submissions, first.

Which was the only way she could have noticed that ad because she never would have gone looking for it on her own. But there it was...

A lifeline thrown out to her in a storm-tossed sea.

4

"Basement studio room with private bath and kitchenette, on Hanover Street. $500 a month, or trade for part-time work, upstairs, at the bakery. Stop by and talk to Jan for more information."

Why, Marion loved Hanover Street! It had the cutest little block of shops and restaurants that resembled some turn-of-the-century European market place. There was always something going on down there, too. They even had a farmer's market on Saturdays, during summer and fall that she had so enjoyed meandering through during her French cooking phase.

Suddenly, she thought what a sunny little piece of heaven it would be to live in a place like that for a while. To turn over the burden of her entire house to some family that could manage it better than she could. When she finally did navigate over to rentals and real estate, and saw how much three bedroom houses, with a den, were renting for...

She grabbed up her car keys and headed straight for *Klinehoffer's Bakery* before anyone else got the same idea. The place was an absolute dream. At least, it seemed like that to Marion, just then. And it was surprisingly easy to nail down, too, because Jan recognized her from the picture that always accompanied her cooking column. Imagine that! Her first ever fan she met face-to-face, and—once, again— the whole thing went off so smoothly it seemed charmed.

In spite of all her desperate behavior and secret suspicions that there might not really be a God up in heaven looking after her. No matter how many years she taught Sunday school. That she might never see Bill, again. Which was really the only reason she kept hanging on to the last shreds of her sanity and trying to resist those dark, terrible thoughts she had been having lately. The fear of which was beginning to pepper her hair all over with gray. Seriously.

It was quite common for people who had been through such a stressful experience to have their hair turn gray. Just look at nearly every man who had stepped into the office of President of the United States. They started going gray from the minute they took the oath and were told all the national secrets. Fear does that to people. Which—like a wolf in sheep's clothing—is what the ugly face of stress really is, if you ever press in and take a good look at it.

Something that can scare the pieces out of you. All of which Marion knew first hand, ever since she started contemplating the idea that her house might be haunted. And not by her wonderful husband, Bill, either. No, whoever her "night visitors" were, they startled and scared the daylights out of her at the oddest moments. As if on a mission to carry out some sinister plot to drive her out of her mind—literally. Which she very nearly believed, considering she had lately even taken to hearing the furniture being moved around in the closed bedroom. No mice on earth were capable of that.

She considered asking Dee to stay overnight, once, with the pretense of working late on the cookbook they were collaborating on. *The Best of Coastal Cookery*, which was a collection of their favorite recipes from the *Columbia Herald* cooking column. She wanted to see if Dee heard any of the strange noises, too. But Marion decided against it at the last moment.

If Dee Parker lost confidence in her sanity, she would have no one on earth she could relate to, at all. Especially since she had estranged herself from all her former friends. For the simple reason that being in the company of happy families almost always set off one of those embarrassing crying jags. Most people had a tendency to avoid her anyway because they felt uncomfortable with the situation and never knew exactly what to say.

All of which gave her the strength to make a snap decision, put her house in the paper, move into that cute little apartment, and start working at the bakery. Immediately. Forget not making any drastic decisions for at least a year—her sanity was at stake. Dee helped her, of course, and even agreed with her. She said she had a good feeling about that cheery little place, painted all over white, with the same yellow-checked curtains and table cloth as in the bakery.

Even the smells drifting down from there were heavenly. It was furnished, too. With a small table and two chairs under the window next to the kitchenette that looked out onto a little walled-in garden area, and a small but comfortable recliner upholstered in the same blue suede as the couch that pulled out into a bed. In the short hallway that led to the bathroom, there was an entire wall of shelves and drawers behind white louvered doors.

No washer and dryer. But as it turned out, there was a set in a room off the bakery kitchen for washing dishtowels and tablecloths that she was welcome to use whenever she wanted. Especially since a portion of her part-time duties was washing the dishtowels and tablecloths. The rest of the time she would be helping to bake all manner of breads and doughnuts. Something she absolutely loved.

Why, it seemed almost as if this lovely little place with its part-time job had been designed especially for her. And in the nick of time, too. Which got her to profusely apologize to God for her attitudes of late, and she considered popping into church next Sunday. It even inspired her to invite Dee over for a home-cooked meal before their next session of work on the recipe book. You could do amazing things with just a crockpot and two electric burners.

"I had no idea you were such a good cook, Marion," she said after her second bowl of Italian vegetable soup with chicken. "We really should include this recipe in the book."

"You think?"

"Definitely. It has a lovely twang to it. What is that?

"A secret ingredient. But, of course, I'll tell you."

Which is just how the darkest days in Marion Bates's life ended. Like a sunrise fading into quiet morning, with prospects of wonderful things in store for the day. No rustlings. No shadows. And quick. Like the flip of a coin... right in the center of God's hand.

"I will bring the blind by a way that they knew not... I will make darkness light before them, and crooked things straight. These things will I do... and not forsake them."

Isaiah 42:16

Anne Lamott

Anne Lamott, who was quoted at the beginning of this story, is the bestselling author of both novels and non-fiction, several of which chronicle her own spiritual journey. Known best for honesty, openness, and humor, she has described beautifully what it means to be "saved by grace." One whose words, though sometimes controversial and often criticized, are always written well.

***

About Lilly Maytree

Lilly Maytree is the author of *Gold Trap, The Pandora Box,* and *The Stella Madison Capers*. Books that sent her careening along on her "Mystery Tours" with her captain husband aboard the *Glory B.* She loves sharing these adventures with readers. It has even been said that she time-travels (but that's probably just a rumor). To find out about her current adventures, simply visit:

www.LillyMaytree.com

Marion's Boston Brown

"It makes a fabulous breakfast bread."

1Tbs butter for greasing

1 ½ cups brown bread flour*

1 tsp baking soda

½ tsp salt

$^{1/3}$ cup molasses

1 cup milk

½ cup dried raisins or cranberries

*Traditionally, brown bread flour is equal parts of wheat, rye, and cornmeal, mixed. However, Marion's variation is to use: 2 (heaping) tablespoons of whole wheat flour, 4 tablespoons of sweet white sorghum flour, 6 tablespoons rye flour, and 6 tablespoons cornmeal, all mixed together to make hers. Which usually comes out to the one and a half cups of brown bread flour required for the recipe.

Instructions For Preparation

Turn crockpot onto high and put water into a teakettle to boil. Generously grease the sides and bottom of a one-pound coffee can (or a large vegetable can if tin is scarce) and remember to remove all paper labels

Combine flour, soda, and salt in a mixing bowl. Stir in the molasses and milk. Fold in the raisins (or dried berries). Fill the can about two-thirds full with batter. Cover the top with foil, and tie securely with string to make airtight. Place in the crockpot, and fill with boiling water to halfway up the outside of the can. Cover with lid, and if there is a steam vent, cover over with a dishtowel.

Let simmer (on high) for 2½ hours. Turn off crockpot and open. Knife inse4rted should come out clean when done. Let cool one hour before slicing.

Toast or serve plain with butter. Also good with cream cheese. Delicious!

Author's Note

Shortly after these events took place, Marion and Dee stumbled upon an adventure that would change both of their lives forever. But that, dear friends, is another story. One which you can learn more about in Lilly Maytree's novel, The Pandora Box, available wherever books are sold. Or visit Lilly's website at www.LillyMaytree.com if you would like a personally autographed copy sent to you. Oh, yes, and you can also read the first chapter at the end of this book.

Thank you for reading this story! May you be specially blessed knowing that you have blessed others simply by doing so.

Other Books by
Lilly Maytree

Gold Trap

Megan Jennings is headed to Africa for high adventure and divine appointments until she makes a small wrong turn. But what is faith, if not to strike out against impossible odds believing you will win? Or leap out into the dark knowing someone will be there to catch you? Someone does catch her... but it isn't who she was expecting.

The Pandora Box

Journalist D.J. Parker learns the location of a famous cache of diamonds that were stolen during World War II. What she doesn't know is—the federal government has been following the case for years. With an old journal to lead the way, she sets out aboard a yacht that once carried the infamous Herman Goering. A thrilling treasure hunt that could either prove to be the adventure of a lifetime... or her worst nightmare.

The Stella Madison Capers...

Home Before Dark
(Caper #1)

Here is the first of the Stella Madison Capers, the story of how everything started, and how she escaped from a catastrophe that seemed to come out of nowhere. Which is the nature of catastrophes but it's so hard to be logical when you're in the middle of one. It's also the story of how she met the colonel (if you're interested in that sort of thing).

A Thief in the House
(Caper #2)

Stella Madison is back, this time with a bevy of friends. But just how far should a person go when it comes to sticking by their friends? There's a thief in the rambling old mansion she moved into. And while it was someone who was quick to lend help when Stella needed it most, how can she possibly return the favor without jeopardizing herself along with them? No person is obligated to go that far... right?

Voyage of the Dreadnaught
collection of four Stella Madison Capers

Here is a collection of the four Stella Madison Capers

covering the entire voyage of the Dreadnaught, through the Inside Passage to Alaska. Includes: *Sea Trials, The Pushover Plot, Lost in the Wilderness*, and *The Last Resort.* Also includes a brief account of Lilly Maytree's true-life voyage along the same route, in the sailboat *Glory B.*

For Writers...
Unspoken Rules

Popular books (those stories everyone likes no matter what the subject) all have certain things in common. And what they have most in common is what they DON'T do. Within the following pages, dear writer, you will find the three most important "don'ts" of popular fiction that I learned when I was studying the masters. Why? Because I love research and I never mind sharing my notes.

Writing Rules!
(a mysterious student handbook)

A mysterious little desktop handbook that can help anyone (well, almost anyone) with writing rules. Especially if you are a student and have to write things all the time.

41

Excerpt from
The Pandora Box
an inspirational adventure novel by
Lilly Maytree

1

The Assignment

*"How will you get me out," I asked my editor, "after I
once get in?"* ~Nellie Bly

It was visiting day at the psychiatric hospital. Dee
Parker sat at her usual table in the lounge, next to a
foot-wide floor-to-ceiling window that allowed only
a narrow view of the outside lawn. No need to attract
attention. It was not an opening window and there
was no way to escape. That word, again. It kept
popping up every time she turned around. Honestly,
if people could read each other's minds they'd all be
staring at her.

Better get a grip. This was the day. The real deal.

She was going to help Nelson Peterson escape from Wyngate State Hospital. Of course, that was not part of her original assignment, and her editor would hit the roof when he found out. But she would deal with that after she got Peterson safely away. For weeks, now, she had only been coming only as far as this visitor's lounge to talk with the old gentleman. But she knew very well what was behind the green double doors that led to the wards. Just the thought of what went on behind them was enough to give her nightmares. But—if all went according to plan—it would soon be over.

Dee felt again for the sprig of miniature roses she had tucked into the band of her straw hat and forced herself not to look around so much (the smell of roses was supposed to have a calming effect on people). There were too many them who were getting used to her weekly visits and might engage in conversation if they caught her eye. Today, of all days, she did not want to stand out, or be remembered. Except there was something troubling in the atmosphere this afternoon. She could sense it.

Probably just her nerves.

She watched an orderly escort a disheveled woman across the room in much the same way a person might take a dog out for a walk, then rather abruptly seat her at a crowded table of waiting visitors. It was Iris Kitner, with an inside-out pajama top on instead of something more suitable that went with her skirt. Hadn't anyone helped her dress today?

The hum of their voices was too far away to make out what anyone was saying but Dee had heard enough past conversations to know things were progressing the same way they did every week. They would all have a lively visit among themselves, with little or no interaction with Iris. Then they would say their goodbyes. After which, Iris would have a few moments of free rein with the complimentary coffee and cookies set up on the long table against the farthest wall before another white-coated somebody took her back upstairs.

Less than five minutes later, she popped up from her chair with an outburst of bizarre babbling and refused sit down, again. Now, that wasn't like her, at all. The plump, forty-something woman (whose auburn ponytail was always crooked) was fairly complacent most Fridays. As if the thought of coffee and cookies was enough to keep her on best behavior.

Which made Dee wonder if these troubled souls might have more sensitivity to otherworldly things than normal people. Something to look into as a possible follow-up story for the series she was writing for the *Columbia Herald*. The headline might read: *Mental Patients: Is What They See Real?* A thought that was interrupted when a self-conscious glance from a teenager in the group collided with hers. Grandson or nephew, who was embarrassed at the way Iris was behaving.

Dee realized she was watching people, again, and forced herself to look away. Instead, she deliberately turned her seat toward the green double doors on the other side of the room and waited. What was taking so long? Did Nelson forget what day this was?

"Come on, Nels," she murmured half-aloud. "You're not giving someone a hard time up there, are you? I don't have nerves of steel like you do. Oh, dear Lord...what if—"

For heaven's sake, Iris had moved into her peripheral vision, again, messing around with the refreshments, already. Dee tried not to watch her. Except when the unmistakable crash of a coffee cup onto the floor (probably full) caused a momentary lull in the hum of visitors.

She had to do something. That sour-faced kitchen worker who should never have been hired for this kind of job was on duty today. In her late sixties, she did not like to clean up messes. Instead, she would complain to housekeeping. Which would cause an even bigger disturbance, and Iris would be returned to her room, early. Meanwhile, the family picnic was going on without her, and none of them seemed inclined to come get her.

So, Dee slung the strap of her purse over a shoulder, picked up her package, and headed over there. But before she even got across the room, Iris stepped on an errant cookie that had also hit the floor, and the inevitable happened. Ms. Sour-face made an immediate exit through the green doors to tell somebody.

"Hey there, Iris, need some help?" Dee filled a fresh cup, piled another assortment of cookies around the saucer and steered her toward the nearest table. The corners of the woman's mouth turned up in a barely detectable smile and she settled down with a contended sigh.

"Cream and sugar?" Dee set a few packets in front of her without waiting for an answer, and then left her package on the table for a moment while she turned back to clean up the mess before housekeeping arrived.

"Miss Parker?" The tap on her shoulder a few moments later gave her a start.

"Was this ever clumsy of me!" She scooped up the soppy napkins and deftly tossed them into the nearby trash bin before turning around. "Slipped right out of my..." She suddenly found herself looking into the magnified eyes of a large-boned, ruffle-haired orderly whom she didn't recognize. Which department had he come from? He had thick glasses, and was wearing a blue uniform instead of the typical white one.

"Mr. Peterson can't come down today," he informed her.

"Oh?" She'd been told her dark blue eyes were fringed with unusually long lashes, and he seemed mesmerized by them. So, she said the first thing that popped into her mind to break the spell. "Shall I go up, then?"

He glanced toward the green doors, first, as if someone beyond might have heard her say that. "No, I don't think you better."

"Well, I would at least like to leave my package." She looked back toward the brown-wrapped bundle she'd left on the table and inwardly cringed when she saw Iris begin to open it. The visitor's lounge was getting more crowded, now, and the place was turning into a hub of confusion. "What room is he in?"

"6B. But Miss Parker, He really isn't up to—"

"Did you say six?" Dee felt a sudden hollow in the pit of her stomach. "Why—that's the violent ward. What on earth is he doing there?" She walked over to collect her package before the contents tumbled out in plain sight.

The orderly followed close behind. "It is often necessary for the safety of our staff, as well as other patients, to confine..." The textbook answer accompanied a complete shutdown of any previous communication between them.

"Oh, honestly." Dee added more cookies to Iris's plate and retrieved the package when the woman's interest shifted. She turned around, again. "There must be some mistake. He has his quirks, but he isn't violent. Putting him in with dangerous people could give him a heart attack! Now, who do I talk to about this?"

When she was met with nothing but a blank stare in reply, she closed her eyes for a moment, sighed heavily, and willed herself to calm down. But it didn't have much effect. The minute she opened them, again, her impatience popped right out her mouth. "Oh, I'll just take care of it, myself!"

Then, she whisked past him, her flowery print dress set in motion with a determined stride. At that pace her yellow heels clicked along the gray linoleum, drawing attention like some bright tropical bird moving through dark forest.

Nearly everyone in the room saw her walk through the green doors.

The Pandora Box

Available from LightsmithPublishers.com,
or wherever books are sold.

For an autographed copy, visit:

www.LillyMaytree.com

If you enjoyed reading this Lightsmith Publishers *"Just A Thought" Story*. please share it with someone. You can also find other inspirational stories by visiting:

www.LigtsmithPuhblishers.com

If you have children, you may even enjoy browsing the *"mysteriously different books"* over at:

www.SummersIslandPress.com

Both imprints are divisions of the Wilderness School Institute, a nonprofit educational organization based in Thorne Bay, Alaska, where they *"take learning back to nature."* You can find more information about them here:

www.WildernessSchoolInstitute.org